CW00853274

CONTENTS

A Brief Introduction   5

His Vision   6

From Human to Animal   8

Psychological Torture   12

Part One: The Beginning of the Tour   16

Promotion   17

Jack and Jill   19

What Jack and Jill Do   22

What Jack and Jill Really Do   26

The Wrath of Jill (and Jack)   30

A Video of Promo For Midnite's Show   34

Big Bertha   38

What Big Bertha Does   41

Part Two: Investor   45

Why Need Money?   46

Mysterious Woman   48

A Famous Man   52

Deeper into the Tour 56

Run, Hamster, Run 59

More Zoo Tour 64

Keepin' it in the Family 67

Part Three: A Turn (For the Better) 70

Business Deals 73

A Short Pointless Walk 77

Blake the Broken Man 80

Part Four: What We Do For Business and Entertainment 84

What's Happenin' 85

Behind Closed Office Doors 90

Part Five: Gratuitous 92

New Friends 93

Always on the Job 96

Sexy Time 98

Small Slice of Promotional Commercial 102

Watching a Woman Work 105

A note from my dark mind 107

**extreme horror
from the dark mind of
Sea Caummisar**

Zoo of People
Extreme Horror

From the dark mind of
Sea Caummisar

This is entirely a work of fiction, pulled out of my own imagination. All characters and events are not real (fictitious). If there are any similarities to real persons, living or dead, it is purely coincidental.

To my knowledge, there is no zoo like this in existence. This story is a figment of my imagination. Fictional.

I do not condone violence (unless it is fictional).

A violent zoo does not sound safe for the participants, so it's a good thing that these characters are not real performers.

In the form of fiction, I do find this zoo to be entertaining.

If it were real life, I would not enjoy it.

This is nothing like the real life human zoos from history.

Also, it's not nice to keep people in cages. Nor is it nice to put them on display against their will. That's what social media is for. People who willingly put themselves on display. Which can sometimes be more entertaining than a zoo. Especially when they act like fools....

A BRIEF INTRODUCTION

A zoo of people.

A new idea for the dark web universe.

People held against their will, filmed and streamed on the internet, purely for entertainment.

The BOSS asks Madam Midnite to help him make a commercial and advertise his newest venture to his dark web viewers.

Also, the BOSS is forming new relationships with new business partners.

Warning: extreme horror. Some gross scenes. Some violent scenes.

HIS VISION

The workings of the dark web grew tiresome.

Sex.

Violence.

Those types of streams had a large viewership, but it felt mundane. Boring. Typical of all dark web channels.

His ways were better.

Fresh ideas to breathe new life into the way people consumed their violence was the better way.

Even his past failures couldn't deter him from probing his mind, seeking out new and creative ways to further his ventures, leading him deeper onto a path of new ways to entertain the masses of people with dark minds.

His 'Experience' show bombed, the viewers not tuned in to watch any more of it.

His 'Circus' was okay, but had many kinks that needed to be worked out due to ill-mannered employees.

Madam Midnite's show, 'My Vagina Smells Like Sulfur', made him plenty of money, and possibly he could monopolize off her if she were to promote his new idea.

A zoo.

A zoo of people.

Not only could he invite his elite members to visit it in real life, but could also stream his living exhibits over the dark web, giving home viewers a chance to enjoy his newest creation.

It would be costly, but most profitable businesses were.

It would take time, money, loyal employees, and patience to pull this off.

But it would be worth it.

His innovative ideas could forever change the dark web.

The boss was a man with a plan.

Several plans, actually.

This was just the beginning.

FROM HUMAN TO ANIMAL

With the help of two psychologists on his payroll, the boss agreed to their plan of ways to mentally break down the humans that would be the exhibits in his zoo.

The first process was surgery to alter their appearances.

There was always a chance that one of his victims would be known by one of the home viewers, and masks were used frequently. It would be bad for business if one of his prominent members logged on and saw a relative or close family friend being used as a victim in his corner of the dark web.

Before kidnapping and/or abducting a person, it was easy to trace all the ties of his Elite members. The ones worth more money than normal people made in their entire lifetime. And it was hugely enforced to check and double check that anyone involved in their shows was not associated with any of the Elites.

It wasn't so easy to do that with the home viewers. Many of them obscured their identities online, making it impossible to know whom they would recognize.

Also, there were too many at-home-viewers to keep track of.

Therefore, masks were an easy solution.

For the zoo, the process would be more detailed.

Once a victim was kidnapped, they were left with no freedoms, no choices, and nothing except their bodies and internal thoughts.

The boss' plan would strip them of even that.

If they were going to be an ongoing long-term exhibit in his zoo, any tattoos, scars, or birthmarks were surgically cut away. New scars would only add an extra layer to their physical appeal as being viewed as animals.

To be humane about the physical transformation, each victim was given anesthesia and asleep when a surgeon removed the flesh of their faces.

The boss watched through a window as a doctor's steady hand used a scalpel to create an incision beneath the victim's chin and curved it upwards of their jaw, to the front of their ears, eventually to the forehead just in front of their hairline.

There was blood, but not as much as the boss expected, making this anticlimactic on the gore scale, but an interesting process to witness all the same.

It wasn't meant to be perfect, and the boss had even used the word 'sloppy' when describing what he wanted as the final result.

After the incision was complete, the doctor used another tool (similar to scissors without pointy tips) to peel the face flesh away from the victim, careful not to tear it.

Fatty tissues and muscle beneath the skin, resembling pinkish clots that reminded the boss of rubbery corn kernels, were revealed. Ornery bumps that are never meant to be seen by the human eye.

With each movement of the doctor's hand, the underlying facial layers jiggled, its lumpy textures wiggling like a firm gel.

Starting beneath the chin, the surgeon peeled away the dermis, epidermis, and possibly some of the subcutaneous, slowly, each tug removing more flesh away from the patient's face.

Until he reached the nose, and created another incision, circular to leave the nasal area intact. Same with the eyes.

Soon, the doctor was holding a solid, thin piece of meat in his hands, what was once the face of the victim. Or at least the superficial appearance of the victim.

Without skin, the victim's face was now gooey and looked so soft. Bright yellows and pale pinks, an array of colors that nobody would ever expect to be buried beneath what made them appear human.

Due to the surgeon's insistence about fear of infection, the doctor was adamant that the skin would have to be reapplied.

It was the boss' idea to cut that superficial

layer into patches and sew them back together, and eventually reattach it to the patient's facial structure. Each patch was to be no more than an inch wide and an inch in height.

The end result was hundreds, possibly thousands of stitches, gluing the top layers of flesh together like a jigsaw puzzle, forever making this victim unrecognizable.

The original circular incision that encompassed the entirety of the original face was now a beautiful tract of raised stitches.

The sutures would leave behind an amazing design of scars.

The exhibits would still be human, just not attractive in the typical sense.

But what the boss saw was beauty. A look he wished he could trademark.

PSYCHOLOGICAL TORTURE

Mental transformation from human to animal was not an overnight procedure. It was long and tedious, and so dangerous that each victim was watched closely by doctors.

To make these people what he wanted, they had to be broken down and rebuilt.

During the healing process, the patients were left alone in pitch black rooms, completely silent rooms, for twenty-three and a half hours a day.

Chained to a table, unable to move, the victims were forced to be alone with nothing but their thoughts, with the hope that anxiety and fear would be their demise.

The silence so annoying that the victims would eventually hear their own heartbeats, the sound of blood flowing through their veins, and maybe even create a constant ringing in their ears. Lack of noise would be a burden to their internal clocks, thoughts, and bodily functions.

Thirty minutes a day was allotted for medical care and feeding, accompanied with a strobe light so bright that it offended their eyesight, the rotation between complete darkness and far too bright light assaulting their senses and confusing them.

A mirror was hung above the victim so they were forced to stare into their newly patched faces, even unrecognizable to themselves. All the victims were allowed to view was their new appearance, a way to force them to accept their new reality.

Their own face, monstrous, staring back at them in the flashes of light.

The doctors were instructed to not speak to the victims, and only check the stitches for infection or anything else that might be a hindrance to the patients.

Within that daily thirty minutes, the catheter bags were changed, allowing more room for their urine to flow within the tubes forced inside their urethrae and punctured into their bladders. Diapers were changed.

Food was not administered orally, but rather via a feeding tube surgically inserted on the side of their abdomens.

The boss needed to keep them alive, but didn't even want to offer them the pleasure of eating food. When freedoms are removed and a person is left with nothing, even a burst of flavors upon their tongue would be considered a luxury.

For now, these people were offered zero frills or indulgences, and only their basic needs were tended to.

After sixty full days of being chained down, enduring silence and darkness (23.5 hours daily), staring at their newly disfigured selves (.5 hours daily), it was time to rebuild them into what the boss deemed as an ideal human animal.

++++

Muscles were atrophied, so physical therapy was a must to resume mobility.

Most of the patients were docile, but a chain was always attached to their ankles, allowing them movement, but only six feet at most.

If a patient didn't do what was asked of them, even if it was the menial task of standing, they were electrocuted with a cattle prod.

Good behavior was awarded, and after a successful physical therapy session, food was given, usually something flavorful and sweet.

Hygiene was tended to with hoses, only cold water used for the first month, reserving hot water as another award for good behavior.

These were human beings, but many chose not to speak, and when they did, it wasn't in complete sentences. Usually, only single words were used to either answer questions or to ask for food.

Physically, they were considered healthy.

Mentally, they were broken and hopeless. Operating on only the basic needs of survival and primal instinct.

Escape was impossible.

Fighting was fruitless.

Even if they did manage to overcome a caretaker or a doctor, the chain ensured they weren't going anywhere.

This was their reality now, and the victims had no choice but to participate in whatever the boss envisioned for them.

PART ONE: THE BEGINNING OF THE TOUR

PROMOTION

"I've always loved the zoo. Animals are nicer than people."

The boss stared into Madam Midnite's hollow eyes, wishing for more of a conversation, hoping that she understood. "Great. But you do know why you're here. Right?"

"Sure," she waved her hand like she was swatting a fly, but she was actually pushing his question away. "Of course I do."

Having worked with Midnite, the boss was well aware that her talent was beauty and not brains. "Then explain it to me."

"Oh, did you forget already?" she asked innocently.

The boss nodded through gritted teeth, his patience worn thin.

"Well, with the dark web zoo being new and all, I'm here to have a look-see and have fun."

"Close enough," the boss said with a grin. "I can't believe it, but your show 'My Vagina Smells Like Sulfur' is the top-rated channel in our dark web division. To convince people to upgrade to a premium subscription and watch 'Zoo of People', you're here to promote it. Your pretty face is the easiest way to separate our viewers from their hard-earned cash."

"Wait, the zoo isn't animals? You said people?"

Outdone with his employee, the boss tried his best to hide his agitation at her lack of comprehension. "We've been over this, multiple times. Why would people watch an animal zoo on live cameras? I've worked hard on this zoo and the exhibits. They're not animals in the typical sense. Humans are animals. Mammals. In the primate sense, yes, they're animals."

Madam Midnite stared at him, a blank expression on her face.

"They're people. A zoo of people."

Midnite's plump lips, recently injected with dermal filler, formed an 'O' shape. "Oh."

The boss spoke simpler to help her get a grasp on the situation. "You sure are pretty. We'll get you on camera touring the zoo. We'll film this, so we can edit later. Very few of our clients will ever visit here in person, however, we'll stream the zoo exhibits over the dark web. You'll be like an influencer and hopefully persuade your viewers to also subscribe to the zoo channel. Got it?"

"So I just walk around and have fun?"

"Sure. We'll get to the scripted stuff later. We'll promote what we record during your vagina show. See if that gets us more views at the zoo."

JACK AND JILL

Madam Midnite leaned forward to read a sign, her superficial, plump, bare breasts centered in the camera lens.

"Jack and Jill," she read aloud. "Those names sound like they go together for some reason."

Behind the sign was a large window, currently covered with a black curtain. "Is this the zoo? I expected a zoo to be outdoors, not in a warehouse. Zoos aren't meant to be inside buildings," Midnite queried with a confused look on her face.

The boss knew that today would be difficult, but had no clue it would be this hard to get Midnite to play into the camera to advertise his newest attraction. "This makes sense. The people here, exhibits held captive, are easier to contain indoors. Easier to care for."

"People? I don't see any people. Only blackness." With a finger, Midnite touched the glass and poked her dim reflection on the tip of her mirrored nose.

The cameraman and the boss exchanged glances, halfway stifling the urge to laugh and the urge to roll their eyes.

"That's a curtain between the window panes. Once we open it, then you'll be able to see inside," the boss explained. A glance at his watch reminded him that he needed to hurry this along. "Why don't you ask me about Jack and Jill before we open the curtain?"

Midnite had no clue that she was being coached, being produced by the boss, to give him the footage he desired.

"What about Jack and Jill?"

"Both attractive. Both members of Sex Addicts Anonymous. Both taken from outside a meeting, actually. I think they'll make for some good entertainment. Especially since we hide medicine in their food to raise their already heightened libidos."

"You mean to tell me," Midnite began, her words excited and rushed, "that you found two people whose names compliment each other so perfectly?"

The boss did roll his eyes. "Yes. Because that makes more sense than changing their names for the exhibit."

"Oh wow!" Midnight was profoundly amazed, her eyes now sparkling. "Can we see them? What do they do?"

All it took was a slight hand gesture from the boss, and somewhere somebody unseen must have hit a switch and the black curtain began to open.

"Pan out, but keep her in the shot," the boss instructed the cameraman. "Naturally, my voice will be dubbed over later, but we'll get to that another time."

Through the glass were two nude beings, one male

and the other female. The enclosure was three walls of cement blocks, high ceilings with cameras in the corners.

Midnite's eyes grew wide as she peered inside, full of questions. "They're sitting there across from each other. Doing nothing. They look weird. What's on their faces? I don't get it."

"They're sitting right now," the boss explained, "and you can't see it very well, but they have chains around their ankles. The chains are controlled remotely, retract to and from the walls, and it's short right now so that they can't touch each other."

"I'm so bored," Midnite said, not taking her eyes away from the window. "I don't get it. Why would people pay to watch this?"

"I'm just thinking aloud, giving you context. For your own commentary." The boss checked his watch. "Feeding time was twenty-five minutes ago. The show should begin anytime now."

WHAT JACK
AND JILL DO

Jill's balanced diet, designed by a nutritionist, kept her body slim, and the natural curves of her bosom, ass, and hips still intact. Make-up wasn't necessary due to patches of flesh sewn into her face, and added an animalistic look.

The boss knew Jill was meant to be sexy and objectified by home viewers to masturbate to her image, but the face was not the focal point of most people who watched pornography.

The boss watched Midnite, who was watching Jack jack off, who was staring holes through Jill.

A noise, something mechanical and off-putting, distracted both parties of the exhibit.

"That's their ankles chains extending," the boss explained. "I'll have to find a way to make them more quiet. I'm still working out some small kinks."

The two human beings on display were reduced to grunts and groans. "Also, for this particular exhibit, their tongues were severed. Some of the human animals we allowed to keep their capability to speak, but not Jack and Jill."

Midnite was no longer paying much attention to the boss' words because she was enthralled by what she was viewing. After the boss pointed it out, it was very noticeable when they opened their mouths that their tongues were short and stubby, barely able to extend to their teeth. A thick row of scarred tissue, a large mass on the tip, presumably from being stitched up.

The patchwork of Jack and Jill's faces was a distraction, but was also doing what it was supposed to do. It made Midnite feel uncomfortable, but made it easier for her to realize these people no longer operated on the same level as normal people.

Jack's penis, thick in girth and long in stature, stood out from his body like a sturdy appendage. An appendage that made Jack groan each time he stroked it.

The human animals, both who couldn't keep their eyes off the other, didn't wait for their chains to extend. Jack and Jill grew impatient and stepped forward, nearing each other, trying their best to stretch the chains that bound them.

At first, it was the tips of their fingers that were touching.

Then they could reach the other's chests, Jack's hands centered upon Jill's mounds of pleasure.

Jill was thoughtlessly trying to sink her fingertips into Jack's bare flesh, trying her best to pull her into him.

The movement of the chain wasn't a fast process, but it didn't stop the human animals from trying to expedite it.

Noises, inhuman sounds, escaping their mouths, expressed their desires. It was evident these two both felt a fire growing between their legs, their minds only concentrating on curing those itches.

It was poetic, in a barbaric way. "What?" Midnite asked. "How? They are human, but acting more like animals."

The boss didn't comment, not wanting to bore her further with the extensive psychological warfare waged against his exhibits. What they were watching spoke for itself.

The exact moment that the chains were long enough, Jack and Jill pressed their bodies together with abandon, no worries about hurting themselves or each other. Their lust was heavy, not needing foreplay to get them excited.

Jill's thighs glistened with her own bodily fluids, a thin sheen of liquid coating her skin.

Using both hands, Jack continued to shove Jill backwards, until she took the hint and laid herself flat on the concrete floor, her legs instinctively spread for him.

Jack wasted no time and offered no kisses or sensual touching.

His only goal was self-gratification.

The man, driven by only instinct, plunged his rod into his mate's moist entry.

Jill didn't mind the weight of his body on top of her.

The camera angles hadn't been perfected yet, and the boss knew that if he was airing this to the dark web, all the home viewers would see was Jack's bare ass, rutting into the woman like a horny sheep.

The boss' mind wondered whether they could find video of animals in the wild, something similar to what they were witnessing between the two human animals. To show the comparison of how truly animalistic these human animals were acting.

All Jill could do was pull the man closer to her body, her teeth even breaking the skin of Jack's shoulder, which didn't detour Jack from his goal of pounding her pussy to completion.

Jack collapsed on top of Jill, his body tired from all the thrusting.

It was over almost as soon as it began.

"That's all?" Midnite asked, disappointed in how the act was hurried and rushed. "I still don't get it?"

The boss held up a single finger. "Wait for it."

Jack pulled away, and rolled off his mate, and the loud clinking started again.

WHAT JACK AND JILL REALLY DO

The chain around Jack's ankle started getting shorter, pulling him closer to the wall.

Jill still laid where she was, one hand rubbing her clitoris and folds of her vagina, her chain unmoving. Two fingers of her other hand inserted into her gash that was dripping with her own and Jack's bodily fluids.

Her motions were haphazard and all over the place.

"Naturally, she isn't pleased," Midnite commented. "His performance was terrible. If a guy did that to me, that quick, I think I'd murder him."

Jack had no choice but to stay near the wall, the chain only inches long. His penis grew erect again, the medicine doing its job. To reach further, Jack laid flat on his belly like a snake, trying his best to extend his arm towards Jill, who was enjoying her alone time with herself.

But she was out of reach.

Jack's grunts and groans sounded painful. The only

thing he wanted was to get near Jill again and thrust his sex organ deep inside her sex cavity. His instincts only wanted his body to feel that pleasure again.

The wall behind them opened, a door so well-placed that it was hidden. No door handle was present, no window, nor a doorjamb; it was painted to blend into the environment.

A man was shoved through the entrance, and the door immediately closed behind him. This man also nude, looked confused and out of place.

"Help! Help!"

"Who is that?" Midnite asked, not daring to remove her eyes from him. "Why's he injured?"

The newly introduced human to the zoo exhibit was covered in bruises, and his left ankle was bent at an unnatural angle, the inner arch of his foot almost parallel with the concrete floor. None of this prevented the man from turning around (mostly on his right foot) and seeing the morbid scene of Jack and Jill.

A naked woman pleasuring herself and a naked man trying to pull his leg free of a chain to reach her. Both faces disfigured, barely resembling people.

It took a few moments before Jill noticed him, but she eyed him up and down, as if her hormones had guided her to the new specimen. A man she could reach. Her mind telling her that maybe this man could offer her the pleasure her body craved.

"That man is repurposed, for lack of a better word," the boss began explaining. "He's a little roughed up from being in another video earlier, some boring violence stuff. They beat him with some wooden boards. Let's see how our human animals respond to him."

Jill's chains clanked behind her as she rushed towards the injured man, jumping onto him, her legs wrapped around his waist, knocking him down.

The new man tried to throw her off of him, but she was an animal in heat, hellbent on getting what she wanted.

"No!" the man yelled. "Lady! What is your problem!"

Upon closer inspection, Midnite noticed that the man's ribs were not only bruised, but one of them was poking through his back, the white of his bone jutting out of his skin. It was no wonder he could barely stand and was hunched over.

Due to the man's weakness, it was easy for Jill to force herself on top of him and knock him down on the ground.

The exposed rib bone chipped as he fell down on top of it, spreading the gash in his flesh even wider.

Unable to breathe, the man's chest rapidly rising and falling was jerking Jill around, who was trying to lower her vagina onto his cock.

His penis was not hard, so no matter how many times she tried to guide it inside of her moist pussy, it frustrated her, obvious by her moaning and grunting and animalistic sounds.

"It's looks like she's trying to fuck some mashed potatoes!" Midnite joked.

And she was correct. It was like trying to fill a hole

of a ceiling with a soft substance, not firm enough to stay inside.

The boss was relieved that her commentary was caught by the camera. His promotion idea might work.

None of the observers were concerned that the man couldn't breathe and was dying.

THE WRATH OF
JILL (AND JACK)

Jill's loins throbbed with an urgency.

All she wanted was to be pleasured, the medicine in her body magnifying her need for sex.

Jack was an option, but he was still chained to the wall out of reach. Past experience had also taught her that he wasn't of much use and all he cared about was getting himself off, ignoring what she needed.

Her knees were straddling the other man, his face now turning blue from where she was squeezing his rib cages too hard with the strength of her legs.

The man tried to fight her off of him, but when he tried to swing his fist at her, his arm dangled at the elbow, as limp as his pecker. Whenever he tried to move, it only labored his breathing more.

Mad at the man for not offering him what she wanted, Jill bared her teeth, practically somersaulting off of him in one swift motion.

Her mouth now around his flaccid shaft, Jill balled

up her fists, pounding on the man's chest like a frustrated child, bouncing off his damaged, purple flesh.

This was another specimen that was of no use to her, angering her beyond belief.

Jill's teeth connected, easily slicing through his penis, blood painting the corners of her mouth like a painted clown's face.

As she pulled away, two squirts of blood fountained from his crotch, the nub of his absent penis a vibrant display of red liquid.

Jill's eyes now on Jack, she charged towards him, her chain snapping her backwards before reaching him.

Jack was stroking his penis with both hands, when Jill spat and the blob of meat struck him on the side of his face.

"What!" Midnite excitedly clapped her hands. "How did you get them to do this? It's so basic, yet unlike anything I've ever seen."

The discarded male genitalia landed in a heap, loose skin wrinkled around the glans like an unraveled manhood.

The loud sound began again, allowing Jack and Jill more chain to reach each other.

Once again, Jack immediately jumped on her and thrust himself inside of her like a jackrabbit.

"I think it's part of their mental breakdowns," the boss answered, "and they pretty much are basic right now. The best part hasn't even happened yet."

Two minutes later, Jack squirted a powerful load

inside his mate and pushed her away, his eyes still now on the dead man.

"This is where it gets interesting," the boss said with pride. "It's not quite jealousy, but more like anger, and Jack wanting to prove himself the alpha or something. I'm sure a psychologist could explain it better," but then he gazed towards Midnite and knew she'd never comprehend complex medical terminology.

Jack's chains were long enough to reach the man's corpse, and his eyes were glazed with harmful intent.

When Jack kicked the corpse and didn't get a response, he flopped down on the man, his fingers spread like claws and his mouth open and ready to bite.

From their side angle, the boss and Midnite watched as the savage, animal-like man sank his teeth into the man's neck and plunged his fingers around the man's torso.

Where the open fracture from the rib bone had split the man open, Jack's paws found entry and started pulling him apart, literally.

The gash spread wider the harder Jack pulled, until stuff that was meant to be inside a human body fell out in clumps and bloody messes. There was no heartbeat, so the blood didn't flow, it trickled along his body, creating a crimson puddle.

Satisfied that Jack had proven his superiority, he smiled through his blood stained lips and walked with his head held high.

"Remarkable, wouldn't you say?" the boss asked.

Midnite was at a loss for words, and it took her a moment to speak. "What happens now?"

"Their chains retract, people come in and remove the dead body, wash Jack and Jill down with hoses. They usually masturbate for a while. Until the next show. Which is usually shortly after feeding time."

The loud clanking sound started again.

The boss held up a finger before turning away. "Jack isn't finished asserting his dominance, yet."

As the chains pulled him away from the dead bag of bones, Jack grabbed his penis and began to urinate on the man he presumed as a threat to his territory.

"He's pissing on him!" Midnite exclaimed. "Classic."

The boss was glad to catch her enthusiasm on camera.

A VIDEO OF PROMO FOR MIDNITE'S SHOW

Sticking with the theme of bodily fluids, a nude Midnite was smiling into the camera lens, only her bare tits and face in the frame.

"Animals and human piss. It's a bodily function, and we all do it," her hands groped the mounds of flesh on her chest, her index fingers rubbing circles around her nipples. "I also know that some of you like watersports."

Unsatisfied that she couldn't remember the script he had written for her, the boss had to remind her what she was supposed to say. "What else do we do?"

Midnite looked confused, until her boss pointed at his backside.

"Oh, yeah," her eyes sparkled. "That's right. Animals and humans piss and shit. Something that we all do. Although I know some of you home viewers enjoy it sexually. Whether it's being pissed on, pissing up inside a woman's vajj, or even drinking it. We can't forget about our scat lovers, either! Anybody out there like some poo in their sex?"

The question was rhetorical, but it was Midnite's way of making her viewers feel special. The space between her ears may have only been filled with empty air and not much in the way of brains, but she had a knack of making people watching her feel important, no matter how unusual their fetish or kink.

The cameraman made some adjustments and zoomed out, the boss watching a screen and in real time what exactly was being recorded.

Midnite's legs were spread, her tanned, tone thighs a tunnel leading to her nude woman parts.

Her shaved vagina exposed, the inner folds of her labia pinkish from a recent vaginal rejuvenation.

The boss admired his employee's dedication to her job, never skimping out on anything that would enhance her beauty. Madam Midnite was many things, amongst those not being very smart, but she was a perfect specimen of female physically, surgically built.

Large breasts with centered nipples; a light brown color areola and pencil-eraser-sized nipples that always seemed to be hard.

Her waist was small, a highlight that gave her body an hourglass shape compared to her hips and chest.

The abdomen area was flat and smooth, laser hair removal to thank for not even having any peach fuzz present.

Plump limps (collagen injected), long luxurious hair (dyed monthly to avoid any showing of the roots of her natural color), contacts (to give her eyes any color she wanted to match her mood), and a strict diet and exercise were the proof of her hard work of being an ideal woman.

No matter how many times the boss had seen her nude, he couldn't help but feel a stir in his libido, and knew it would be the same for the home viewers, male and female, no matter their sexual orientation.

Midnite's body screamed SEX.

The boss watched the screen, Midnite sitting on top of a glass box, clear, with an opening in the top directly below her sex parts.

"Who likes watching that yellow stream directly from the source?" Midnite teased, still playing with her titties.

While still speaking, she started to urinate, the camera catching every bit of it through the glass box. "Who wants me to piss on them? Who would like to drink my urine? Who would lay down like a good little slave and let me sprinkle my tinkle on them?"

Midnite may have turned the boss on when he looked at her, but urophilia and golden showers never interested him. There was still something hypnotic that put him into a trance as he watched the amber puddle collect in the bottom of the glass box.

In his mind's eye, the boss envisioned home

viewers stroking their hard cocks or fingering at their clits while watching this video.

"You think this is hot? Wait until you meet Big Martha. The next exhibit we'll be visiting on our tour day," Midnite stopped peeing and looked at the boss. "How was that?"

"Well, her name is Big Bertha, but I'm sure we can do some edits later. Any chance you could do something for our scat fans? Maybe later we could give you a laxative or something?"

Midnite smiled.

BIG BERTHA

"How much does she weigh?" Midnite asked.

"A little over eight hundred pounds, the last we checked. But due to the diet we're feeding her, it could be more now."

It was the same set-up as Jack and Jill's, the observers looking inside a concrete room through a glass window.

Bertha was perched on the same type of glass Midnite sat upon in the last scene they filmed, just many times larger.

Bertha's knees were bent, ripples and folds of flesh hanging from her legs like jowls. This woman was also nude, but her thighs were so large that they blocked the view of her vagina. Her large stomach rested on top of her thighs, and overflowed on the sides, drooping to the ground.

"Just one of her ankles is larger than both of my thighs put together!" Midnite boasted of her physical fitness.

Two breasts laid over the rolls of her belly, hung loose and low, gravity playing a major factor, nipples tucked beneath and out of sight.

Even her armpits were bulged with fat, causing her arms to stick out away from her body.

What was once a neck was what appeared to be multiple chins, three at least, possibly even four.

Her hands were tiny in comparison to the enormity of her arms, and it felt disproportionate.

A chain kept the woman in place for added security, but the workers doubted the woman would walk away anyway.

"We found her through a tip. An ambulance worker who posted online that she was immobile and wouldn't fit in an average sized car, so it was their duty to transport her to and from doctor appointments."

Midnite nodded, but didn't respond.

"We put her through the same rigorous process as the other animals, apparent by the fleshy patchwork of her face, and feed her. Constantly. Which seems to keep her happy."

The arms that looked too short for her body, but stout, brought a fried turkey leg to her mouth and she chomped into the meat.

Beneath the woman, was the same glass type of box that Midnite used as a toilet, but this one hadn't been cleaned out and was full of yellow liquid and brown solids.

"So that's poop floating in there? Floating in the piss?" Midnite asked. "I'm so glad we can't smell it," she said, laughing.

"That's where she lives now. We never move her. She sleeps sitting up, and eats almost literally all waking day. Sixteen hours a day, at least. Her 'toilet tank'", the boss used finger quotes around his words, "can hold up to five-hundred gallons of bodily waste. Approximately five and a half feet wide, same in width, and five feet tall. Think of it as a see-through septic tank."

"Is that safe? As in clean?" Midnite asked.

The coherent question threw the boss off guard. It wasn't something he expected from his employee due to it being partially intelligent. "Probably not. We do hose her off from time to time, but no, I doubt it's clean. We do have doctors that check her for open wounds and the such, to treat against infection."

Midnite didn't respond, and kept staring at this woman who lived on the glass toilet.

"I'll probably start taking wagers on her weight, like allowing the home viewers to guess her weight. Maybe weekly. Maybe monthly. Also, we'll probably take bets on how long until she dies. Maybe a heart attack? Maybe not? I haven't decided just yet. We could also let home viewers gamble on how many gallons she fills the tank each week. This can be very profitable for me."

"Is that it?" Midnite asked. "I'm sure she does something else, right?"

"Wait for it," the boss said with a smirk. "Showtime is starting soon."

Midnite clapped her hands with excitement and jumped up and down.

WHAT BIG
BERTHA DOES

"Did I mention that we sprinkle her food with an appetite stimulant and other things?" the boss asked. "Dependent on what kind of show we want. Just to see what happens."

Bertha gnawed at the turkey leg, her baby-like arms struggling to get the food into her face hole. Most of the meat was gone, but that didn't stop her from grinding her teeth into the bone, trying to get more food and more flavor. Slobber leaked from the creases of her lips, tainted with greasy residue.

Midnite stared too hard at the large woman's teeth, noticing how yellow they were, and some were even chipped and loose. "There are so many gross things about this part of the zoo."

From behind Bertha, a large man, masked and wearing a long, black trench coat, reached around with his freakishly long arms and took the turkey leg from her, having to forcefully pry it away from her needy fingers.

The woman opened her mouth and squalled at him, but other than her neck, she didn't dare move. Or maybe she just couldn't move. It would require too much energy to make her limbs mobile, and the reward wasn't worth it if it didn't result in food.

The worker was quick about his work, and it looked like he had done this many times before.

It was less than two seconds after he took her food away from her, that he handed her a new item.

Big Bertha, wanting nothing but to feed, didn't even bother to look at what she was handed. It was as if her hand was moving on instinct, and raised it to her frothing mouth to sustain her constant hunger.

"Like I was saying," the boss continued. "We do give her pills to keep her hungry, buried in her food, amongst other types of medications."

"Wha- wha- what?" Midnite stammered, her eyes practically popping out of her head. "What is that?"

The boss didn't reply, but instead used hand motions for the cameraman to catch this authentic moment of disbelief on camera, to help with future commercials for the zoo.

What Bertha was holding had a tail, and her fingers made a perfect loop around its wrinkled skin.

"It's a rat. Shaved. Dead of course."

Not a thought in her head, other than eating, Bertha brought the deceased animal to her mouth, her stained teeth crunching into the side of its head, and one of its front legs. The tiny leg snapped away easily like a twig, but her bite wasn't strong enough to tear the flesh, so she had to pull it away with her arm, the skin stretching until it broke.

Then she chewed, thick black blood foaming from her lips and down the side of her wrist.

"She doesn't care what she's eating?" Midnite laughed at the absurdity of what she was watching.

The boss held up a single finger. "Wait for it…"

Even being on the other side of the glass, the trio heard a gurgling from Bertha's belly, like a thundering continuous boom.

At that time, Bertha's bowels released a steady stream of liquid and some brown chunks leaking from her backside, through the upper hole of the makeshift toilet.

The chocolate-y body fluid collected with the other human waste in the septic tank.

Bertha continued to gnaw at the animal, the fact that she was defecating not hindering her ability to eat.

"Oh, yeah. The rat was also injected with a super fast-acting laxative." The boss was proud of his exhibit, knowing this was something that no other dark web channel offered. "Thoughts?"

"If I didn't have a reputation to maintain, I think I'd gag," Midnite said with embarrassment. "But not me. I'm a true professional."

"That brings me to my next thing. This isn't cheap. None of this is cheap. Zoos cost money to operate. Animals cost money to feed, house, and care for. Medical expenses and such. I'm trying to bring an investor on board. And a new employee. I thought maybe you could help me with that, too."

PART TWO: INVESTOR

WHY NEED MONEY?

Sitting in the office, no cameraman around, it was just Midnite and the boss.

"An investor? Meaning?"

Her question was so innocent, but the boss was pretty sure she wouldn't know the meaning of the word, so he obliged. "Usually, investors pay for part of a business to generate more revenue," the boss stopped talking, realizing he was talking over her head. "An investor would give me money, so we can make more money in the long run, together."

"But you have more money than anybody that I know. I thought you were making tons of money off the gambling and the subscription viewers and all…"

The boss thought she may have continued her thought, but she didn't. "Yeah, that's true, but investors mean more than money. They mean networking, also."

"Networking? Like what computers do?"

The boss didn't hide his sigh. "Sort of. This is someone that I want to be my business partner, not only for the zoo or my dark web stuff, but also other doors they can open for me. I have money. Now I crave the spotlight. There's a couple of people that can help me with that."

"Open doors? None of this is making sense."

"I know," the boss agreed. "All you need to know is that this investor and new employee are fans of yours. They want to meet you, and also get to know my business a bit, so maybe we can start another venture together."

"A fan wants to meet me! That's exciting!" Midnite bounced in her chair, giddy like a child that got a pony for a present, and the boss wished she hadn't dressed. Her intelligence level was low, but she sure was pretty to look at.

"Yes. She's a huge fan. And this woman fascinates me on many levels. Plus, we can help each other. The man, he's easy. All men love you. That's all you need to really know." The boss turned around and poured an amber liquid in a thick glass, mumbling under his breath. "I think that's all you can comprehend for now, anyway." Then he spoke loud enough for her to hear him. "Would you like a drink?"

"Absolutely. I like being relaxed when I meet fans! I don't get to do that very often, since we're not exactly open to the public."

The boss hoped this would work out in his favor.

If it did, it could mean an even brighter future for him.

MYSTERIOUS
WOMAN

Her hair was as dark as the black of night, not natural. It was dyed.

Her skin was clear, her make-up allowing for a paler complexion than her own.

From head to toe, she wore all black, form-fitting clothes. Slacks tailored especially for her, and a pleather blouse that covered her neckline.

Large sunglasses hid her eyes, giving her an even more unsettling look, a mysterious air about her, following her like a brewing storm cloud.

Midnite couldn't contain herself, her eyes tracing the woman's slim frame. The thing about Madam Midnite was that she had so much self-esteem that she never felt inferior to another female, but even she couldn't deny that this woman was beautiful.

Just in a way different from her own.

No fake breasts.

Natural lips, not altered by Botox or a surgeon's hand.

This woman slinked instead of walked, but it was evident this woman didn't love herself as much as Madam Midnite by the way she tried to hide her body with dark clothing and large, black sunglasses.

As if she were an old friend, Midnite stood to greet her, an arm on each of the woman's shoulders, to examine her closer. "I hear you're a fan. It's an honor to meet you."

"Huh?" the woman muttered. "I thought I was the one that was supposed to say that."

"Despite what you may think of Midnite, or whatever your perceptions of her may be…" the boss let his words linger while he thought of the proper word. "She's very innocent. Naive."

The woman redirected her attention to Midnite, whose long fingernails were now puncturing her faux leather shirt. "Likewise."

"That means you like me?" Midnite asked.

The woman looked to the boss, at a loss for words. "Indeed it does. I'm Miranda."

The boss offered her a drink, which gave the woman a chance to break the physical link between her and Midnite, and she sat.

"I haven't had the chance to tell Midnite too much about you, which I thought I would allow you to share, or not share, as much about yourself as you're comfortable," the boss offered, and then he also sat down. "That's up to you. I just promised you that you'd get to meet Midnite, so here she is."

"I'm so flattered," Midnite interjected. "I feel like we're friends already. And I love your style."

That almost got a smile from Miranda, the upward curvature of her face looking foreign and out of place, like she rarely used those particular facial muscles. "I know many people, but don't have many friends, and even a few gimps. Perhaps I'm a stigma. Marked with disgrace. My full name is Miranda Dahmer."

"If you truly feel that way," the boss said, sipping from his glass, "you're at the right place. We have nothing but respect for you and your family name."

Midnite pinched her bottom lip between thumb and index finger and stared off into space. "Dahmer. Dahmer. Why do I know that name? It feels familiar."

Miranda clasped her hands in her lap, looking away. "From what I've been told, I was almost named Phoenix, which would have been a much cooler name than Miranda. Anyway, my father is Damon. Damon Dahmer."

Midnite pulled her fingers away from her mouth and snapped them together, to demonstrate that a thought hit her. "Your dad created that Reality TV show! Easy Money something or another? Where someone actually died on live TV. That man is a legend. That's a classic show."

Some of the gloom surrounding Miranda seemed to dissipate. "Yes. That's him."

The boss smiled, knowing the two of them would get along perfectly. "You two girls keep right on chatting, we're waiting for one more person. And don't worry Miranda, I assure you our next guest is pretty much as private as you. If not even more so. We'll all get along famously."

The boss chose that last word on purpose.

"Famously? Like, we'll get along like celebrities do? I didn't think they got along. I thought they gossiped about each other all the time?"

Miranda looked at Midnite, expecting a laugh from her, but it never came.

"Like I said before," the boss said with a sigh. "She's so innocent. But even half-wits are good people."

A FAMOUS MAN

The boss waited patiently for his next guest to arrive, while Midnite asked Miranda a million questions about her dad and his show.

"Actually, I'm thinking of rebooting a similar show to my dad's," Miranda said, easily opening up to one of her internet idols. "Television rules aren't as strict in this day and age. I think I could pull it off. With some help." Her eyes looked at the boss.

"I feel I've dominated the dark web. Why not try and get into television, too? I have plenty of tech experts that keep my identity hidden, so I don't see that being a problem. I'm thinking fame would feel good on me. Some sort of recognition for my hard work," and then he gave Miranda a wink. "Or perhaps we- me and you - could work on a similar show for the dark web? Or maybe for even what I call the well-lit web. The version everyone can view. There'd be more rules than the dark web, but not as many rules as television."

Miranda chewed her lip. Deep in thought. "Decisions, decisions."

"Oh," Midnite said, in a low tone, snapping her

fingers again. "Networking."

The boss pointed at her. "Exactly. Same as Miranda could help me with ideas for the dark web, and maybe even my zoo. I found her when she used some of her father's money to buy a sexual slave from me on one of my dark web channels. It's kismet."

"Sex slave. Gimp, according to some modern media. A submissive. Call it what you want, but I call it a great outlet for my emotional frustrations."

Midnite stared at the woman, unsure what they were talking about.

There was a knock on the door, and a security guard opened the office door, with a guest.

"OH MY GOD!" Midnite screamed, hands on her cheeks with an open mouth. "Trick Haynes? THE PATRICK HAYNES! Here? Right now? In this room? With us? How did this happen?"

The boss knew this would be a treat for his employee, but didn't suspect her to be so loud and embarrassing. His plan of using Midnite as a pawn, offering Miranda and Trick a chance to meet the biggest star of his dark web channels, could backfire due to her overenthusiasm.

Midnite rushed towards the man, wrapping her arms around him, her face so close to his that she was practically drooling on him. "The king of comedy! The master of jokes! The man who survived a tragedy and makes a living off of telling jokes about death! And sexist jokes. Right? I'm so proud to meet you!"

If Trick had looked uncomfortable, the boss

would have pulled her away from him, but the comedian pressed his body into hers, his pelvic area pronounced. Naturally, most men would die for a hug from Madam Midnite, and a chance to touch her sexy body.

"This is pretty neat," Miranda said so low that nobody else heard her. It wasn't in her nature to draw attention to herself.

"I have other nicknames for him, mostly a very popular screen name, and have dealt with him many times in the virtual world," the boss couldn't help but smile at his accomplishments. "Is this a dream team or what? Imagine what all of us could do together, professionally speaking. Whether on a mainstream channel, or hidden behind the servers of my dark corner of the internet."

"The pleasure is all mine, Madam. I want to wear you like a pair of sunglasses. One leg over each ear."

The boss didn't mind that Trick didn't reply to his comment. How could he expect him to when Midnite was physically throwing herself at him.

"Huh?" Midnite cocked her head. "If you sat down, I think it'd be easier. I could try. But I don't think I could do that standing up. And I don't think you could see through me like sunglasses. There's also no sun in here."

Trick gave the boss a look of confusion. "Is she being for real? I did take a survey the other day that said one out of three women are just as dumb as the other two."

Miranda and the boss both nodded uncomfortably,

unsure what to say.

"What time do you get off tonight?" Trick didn't give her a chance to answer. "Can I watch?"

Midnite scratched her head. "We don't really have a schedule. We do our job, then we're done."

"You really don't get it?" Trick asked.

Miranda and the boss both got a laugh out of that one.

"Who wants to see a zoo of people?" the boss asked. "And after, maybe we could all have a sit down and a few drinks."

DEEPER INTO
THE TOUR

"I guess we started before y'all got here," Midnite stated. "We were filming, though, and the boss has a strict rule about not having any cameras on while you two are around. Safety and privacy or something. But I've seen two nymphos having rough sex, and an over-eater who lives on a glass toilet."

Trick puffed out his chest. "I only know of one sure way to stop a nymphomaniac from having sex."

"How?" Miranda asked, instantly biting her tongue, wishing she had stayed quiet. The long hallway of pure white walls and the brightest fluorescent lights she'd even seen made her feel like she was on display. If only she'd stayed quiet, she could have faded into the background behind Trick and Midnite's larger-than-life presences.

"Marry her!" Trick laughed out loud at his own joke. "What's the difference between a nymphomaniac and a broom closet? Only two men can fit inside a broom closet at once!"

The boss, following behind the group, rubbed his temples and questioned whether he was capable of spending some time with the comedian. Maybe his jokes were funny, but today was about business and not pleasure.

It seemed that Trick took nothing seriously.

Miranda on the other hand was reserved and quiet. Didn't make a fool of herself. And she had a burning passion in her heart to follow in her father's footsteps. The boss respected that.

"If I may," the boss spoke loud enough for all three of them to hear him.

"The zoo isn't officially streaming yet. We're working out some kinks, but I'd love for you to take a look for yourself at some of the exhibits for yourself. My way of proving that I'm capable of more than sex and violent videos.

Whether it be TV, or the normal internet, Miranda's ideas, and Trick's famous personality, we'd have a hit show in no time. And I'd love nothing more than to be involved in that."

Miranda had to look over her shoulder to see the boss, but she was chewing her lip, unsure how to respond. Her facial expression wasn't a happy one.

She never got a chance to respond due to Trick.

"Hey Midnite! Do you have a shovel? Because I am digging you. Did I tell you that I called the rape advice hotline last night? Turns out it was only for victims." Trick laughed after every annoying joke.

"Oh, poor baby," Midnite replied. "So they didn't help you?"

"A woman told me yesterday that she wouldn't have sex with me if I was the last man alive. But then I asked her, 'who would be around to stop me'?"

Midnite stopped walking and scratched her head. "I don't get it."

Midnite continued to walk, leading Trick away, with an extra wiggle in her hips, giving him something to look at. "Is that like a knock-knock joke? It doesn't work unless I ask. So who would be around to stop you if you were the last man on earth?"

Miranda and the boss both rolled their eyes, while Trick laughed.

Midnite couldn't figure out why.

RUN, HAMSTER, RUN

"As you'll see, we keep our animals' identities hidden, and I'll go into detail about that later."

The boss stood in front of a window while the other three looked past him into the room. Concrete walls and floors, bright lights, cameras on the other side filming the action.

"I like to compare this to more of a pet type animal than a zoo type animal, but an animal all the same." The boss stepped aside, giving them a better view, but noticed that Trick was more interested in looking at Midnite.

"Did you hear the one about the guy who worked at the morgue?" Trick asked, speaking quickly so as not to give anyone time to answer? "He told me they pulled a body out of some old nasty lake, and her clit was just like a pickle. I asked him if that was because it was green, and he told me 'nope, it tasted sour'. But Madam, I have to admit, I bet you taste sweet."

Midnite blushed, accepting the compliment, not

sure whether she should laugh or not.

Miranda showed her disapproval by rubbing the side of her face and ignoring the comedian. "What is that?" she asked, pointing. "Some kind of wheel or something?"

Her index finger was aiming towards a large, circular object attached vertically on the wall.

"If I may have your attention, Mr. Haynes, and your patience, Ms. Dahmer. All will be revealed momentarily," the boss spoke loud to cover Trick's laughter. The boss nodded, towards someone unseen behind the black dome of a camera mounted on the ceiling.

A door on the far side of the room opened, and in walked a masked man, dressed in all black, holding a leash attached to a nude man's neck. A third man followed behind them, this one holding a long item in his right hand, and a handgun in his left.

The nude man's head was drooping with his chin towards his chest, and his shoulders slouched. "Please," he begged weakly. "Please no. Don't."

One of his captors brought the long item up to his bare flesh, a cylindrical stick of some sort, and a flash of light and a zapping sound caused the nude man to flinch. A black burnt area developed on his skin and the nude man doubled over.

"A simple cattle prod," the boss explained. "Just enough pain to provide motivation."

After up righting himself, the nude man stepped up inside the circle attached to the wall, the contraption tall enough for him to fully stand.

The man with the gun, and the man with the leash stepped out of the way, and the circle started spinning.

The nude man had no choice but to run to keep up with the momentum of the floor spinning beneath his bare feet.

"I used to have a pet hamster," the boss explained. "I'd spend hours watching him run in his hamster wheel. His tiny feet scampering to get his daily exercise."

"Faster!" the man with the gun yelled, prompting the other security guard to press a button.

The human-sized hamster wheel sped up, the nude man's legs scrambling to keep up with the pace.

"Imagine watching a human doing the same as my hamster. People placing bets as to how fast and how long he can run. We do have a rotation of human hamsters, so this could be an ongoing internet stream."

"Faster!" the gunman yelled again, the other man pressing a button again.

"Of course, for our entertainment, I've hurried things along for us." the boss chuckled.

The wheel was spinning so fast that even though the nude man's legs were running in quick succession, he couldn't keep up. Using his hands, he tried his best to balance himself, to compensate for not running as quick as the wheel was turning.

The nude man fell forward, face-planting into the moving metal, his nose cracking against the floor of the vicious circle, centrifugal force pressing his body into the curved wall.

Blood leaked from his face, and his wrist bent sideways, his loose hand flapping like a flag blowing in the wind.

The circle didn't stop moving, so it brought the nearly lying down man backwards, his stomach curved to mold the shape, his legs now above his head.

Another partial rotation and his body clung to the metal, until his feet were on the highest arc of the dome, and his head at the lowest.

The man's body crumpled, like a sock in a dryer, folding over himself backwards and upside down, his own feet kicking him on the backside of his head.

Gravity took over, his body weight holding him down, the metal inner wall chaffing the bare skin of his chest like a magnified carpet burn.

The gunman laughed audibly, his chortles echoing through the glass window.

Nobody attempted to stop the motion of the wheel, leaving the man flopping at the bottom, screaming out each time one of his fragile bones collided with metal and snapped like twigs.

It wasn't until the boss nodded that another button was pressed, and the thudding eventually stopped due to the slowing of the movement.

The nude man didn't attempt to stand, and groaned in a bloody heap of mangled body parts and instant purple bruises. The right arm at a perpendicular angle, the wrist twisted sideways, and his fingers hardly twitching.

"Shame," the boss noted. "It appears he may have broken his back. It can't be healthy for his legs to lie so limply atop his buttocks."

Trick opened his mouth to speak, but shut it.

Now it was Miranda who was smiling.

MORE ZOO TOUR

The boss led them further down a hallway.

"This next exhibit, one of the few I'd like to make notice, that we didn't make any attempts to hide their identities. Mostly due to them," then he used finger quotes, "'living off the grid'. Meaning, nobody knows them or will miss them anyway."

Trick was quiet, and the boss hoped it was due to him asking him to pay more attention to the tour.

Miranda, on the other hand, was overly excited, causing even her to speak. "Interesting."

Stopping in front of the next window, Midnite stood closest to the glass, ready to see what was next. Trick lingered behind her, his eyes staring at the sexy vixen's backside.

A curtain rolled away, revealing two nude human animals.

The woman, much younger than her male counterpart, turned around to stare back at them through the window.

"She looks-" Miranda's sentence, left unfinished, wasn't a shock.

They were all thinking that something was off, but

couldn't be sure what it was.

Midnite was the next to ask. "You said you didn't alter their appearance?"

"We did not," the boss said with pride. "Didn't have to."

The nude woman, who appeared young by her firm tits and tight skin, had a scrunched up look on her face. Wrinkles, like ripples around her gaping mouth, magnified that fact that she was a mouth breather. Her eyes, one black and the other brown, looked in opposite directions, each towards the corresponding ear.

Her ears hung loosely from the side of her head, one larger than the other, the tops of them not rounded but rather squared.

The nude woman's skin was bruised in places, mostly around her wrists, drawing attention to the fact that she only had four fingers on one hand, each digit the exact same length.

"She has nice tits though," Trick said. "Pussy ain't too bad either. But what is wrong with her?"

Miranda removed her eyes from the exhibit to flash the comedian a glare of disapproval. "She's laying down. Is that club foot? The way her ankles are rolled inward. Can she even stand?"

"They were the hardest to find," the boss began explaining. "He's just a normal guy, right? Nude. Thin. In his fifties. Almost always has an erection."

"What are we looking at here?" Midnite asked.

"They were found in a log cabin, at the top of a mountain. It's quite complicated, but the short version is that man is her father and her grandfather."

Midnite scratched her head. "That's not even possible. How can that even happen?"

Miranda looked away, almost ashamed of herself for gawking. "They've been reproducing from the same gene pool. I'm assuming that man had a daughter, got that daughter pregnant, and the female we're looking at is the product of incest."

"You're correct," the boss confirmed. "The girl's mother, his daughter, didn't survive the abduction, unfortunately. That's all we know ultimately, but further incest is suspected. They can be fun to watch."

The man on display didn't care that he was being watched. His cold eyes didn't waste any time looking back through the window. His hand was stroking his dick, a bit of pre-ejaculate shining on the head of his shaft, which he used as a lubricant.

The woman, flat on her back, a twisted hand to her mouth as if she were trying to suck a thumb that never existed, wobbled her head around between her father/grandfather and the people watching her.

"I assure you, our doctors speculate the woman is at least twenty years old, however, her mental age is much lower."

KEEPIN' IT IN THE FAMILY

The older man ignored the eyes on him and mounted his daughter, his bare ass in the air towards the window. His hands violently gripped her wrists and pinned them to the concrete on both sides of her head.

Next began the pelvic thrusting, his rock hard boner penetrating her vaginal opening like a rig drilling for oil.

The sounds that escaped the deformed woman's mouth-mostly oohs and aahs- weren't typically associated with pleasure, but also didn't discern that she wished for him to stop.

It wasn't passionate, this was pure lust, pure animalistic instinct, but the man did bend his neck down to her face and licked her cheek; the rough sand papery texture of his moist orifice leaving a gleam of wetness of her skin.

"This is it?" Trick asked. "It's like being at a real zoo. Animals screwing, not for performance or a show, but because they want to."

"That very well could be the first intelligent thought you've had all day," the boss mocked. "This exhibit here is trained. They know they get rewarded after trying to reproduce. I'd love for her to get pregnant and see what the next baby would be like. My doctors have assured me that they're both capable of reproducing."

Patrick puffed out his chest, and almost responded but thought twice and chose not to.

Miranda snickered, but quickly covered her mouth.

The sex was boring to watch, but it was over quickly.

A door opened on the far side of the room, and a body was shoved inside the room of the exhibit. "See, a reward."

"I don't get it?" Midnite said.

"Most things you don't darling," the boss responded. "Did I mention their dietary habits on that mountain weren't like ours?"

The man dismounted his daughter, a sticky string of goo stretching between his pecker and her snatch, that popped like a bubble after enough distance.

The man grabbed the dead body, yanked it by its limp arm, and drugged it towards his daughter.

At the same time, both of them sunk their teeth into opposite arms of the corpse, their mouths pulling away with blood around their lips and a chunk of meat in their mouths.

"He brought her the food. Like a parent. He's taking care of her," Miranda said in a hushed tone.

"Yes, you're correct. I like to do business with people who are capable of forming thoughts."

Miranda knew that was an insult towards Trick, and probably even Midnite, but didn't say it aloud.

"I'm undecided what to do with these two, other than hoping for another baby," the boss said, walking away. "Follow me. There's more to see."

The boss led the way, and Trick frowned towards Miranda, who shrugged.

"He's the one that asked for me to be here today," Trick whispered to his female colleague. "He wants to do business with me. Don't you forget that. And don't be trying to make me look bad in front of him."

"What?" the boss turned around. "I'm sorry. I didn't catch that."

"Oh, nothing," Trick smiled coyly. "Nothing at all."

Miranda bit her lip.

Midnite scratched her head.

Trick scratched his balls.

The boss led the way.

PART THREE: A TURN (FOR THE BETTER)

"Did I hear you say you have insight on how to improve the zoo?" the boss kept walking, but made his voice boom with authority. "After all, I'm the one who invited you here today, so I do value your opinion and thoughts."

Miranda put a little pep in her step, relieved that the boss had heard how Trick spoke to her.

Trick smiled like a child who just won an award. It was a toothy grin, one too wide, that annoyed those who didn't win. "Well, I'd sell tickets to have sex with her."

"With who?" Midnite asked, her usual clueless expression on her face. "That incest woman? But doesn't that defeat the purpose? Aren't we trying for more incest babies?"

The boss stopped walking right before a corner. "Mr. Haynes, I believe even Madam here figured that one out. Any other suggestions? Also, let's not include bringing anyone to the zoo. Very few of the elite will ever visit, and we won't subject them to the dangers of our exhibits."

Four people, standing still in a hallway, three sets of eyes looking to Trick for an answer.

The comedian cleared his throat and his face turned red. "What's strong enough for a man, but made for a woman?"

No one answered.

"The back of my hand!" Trick raised his arm in a mock attempt to slap at Midnite. "C'mon, it's just a joke!"

The boss diverted his attention to Miranda. "I value your input. Highly. I agree to my end of the bargain, as long as you will honor yours."

All Miranda had to do was nod.

"What are you talking about? Did I miss something?" Midnite asked.

Trick rolled his eyes. "No, you didn't miss anything except Miranda brown-nosing the boss. She probably sucked his dick or something before the tour."

"I assure you that no such thing occurred," the boss said calmly, and turned the corner. He opened a door, revealing an empty office with nothing except a table and four chairs. "Midnite, if you'll please entertain Mr. Haynes briefly, while Miranda and I have a word in private."

Trick wasn't pleased about feeling left out, but that didn't stop the sexy temptress from grabbing his hand and leading him into the office. "Sure. Fine by me."

BUSINESS DEALS

"There's more to the tour, right?" Trick asked, his eyes on Midnite's overflowing cleavage.

"I'm pretty sure of it. I believe a farm was mentioned at one point, and some other stuff. So I don't think we've seen it all."

"You know what I'd like to see?"

"What?"

"You. No clothes. No nothing. Just me and you, talking about the first thing that pops up." Trick made his way towards her, pinning her against the wall.

"I am at work," Midnite said, scooting her back down the wall and bending herself beneath his arm to get out of his grasp. "I'm not saying no. I'm just saying not right now."

"Oh, I'm sure of that," Trick said, spinning around to face her. "I doubt you ever say no. Especially to someone like me. Do you know how much pussy I've got since I became a celebrity? Pussy here, pussy there, pussy everywhere. Like it's on tap, always flowing for me. I get more ass than a toilet seat."

She took a few steps away from him, towards the

door. "Well, maybe I'll say no now. I don't want to catch something that soap can't wash off."

The door opened, the boss entering first. "What's happening in here?"

Trick shrugged, and Midnite stood close to the boss. "Nothing."

"Is he making you uncomfortable?" Miranda asked. "It's okay to tell us if he is."

"Nothin' I can't handle," Midnite said with a smirk. "I just told him that I'm working, and I'm trying hard to be professional. My boss asked me to play nice, and I am."

"Nice, but that doesn't mean you have to have sex with him," the boss suggested. "I'd never ask that of you, would I?"

"No, I don't think you would."

"Good," Miranda verbalized. "I do like screening my potential business partners."

The boss extended his hand, and Miranda wrapped hers around it and shook it up and down. "Let's make this official."

"What'd I miss when you two were out there talking?" Trick asked, his eyebrows raised. "Are we going through with the reality show? I'd be the perfect host for it."

Miranda held a stun gun in her other hand, and didn't give Trick a chance before pressing it into his chest and squeezing it, sending volts of electricity through his body.

The comedian's body collapsed to the floor, thrashing like he was having a seizure.

Midnite's mouth fell open. "What is happening?"

"I know Miranda is always looking for new sex slaves, so I offered her the best one ever. A misogynist. A gift from me to her," the boss said. "Does this mean the reality show is a go? Your name, my connections. We'd have a hit television show in no time."

"It's a deal. I hate that douche. I'll have some serious fun with him."

"But I thought you said that Trick did some other stuff for you on the dark web?" Midnite asked.

"Oh, he used to, but he's also cocky and likes to run his mouth. I'll admit, Trick Haynes disappearing off the face of the earth does help me, too, but I think Miranda has more of a use for him than I do. This way, I don't have to worry about his loose lips sinking my ship."

The boss opened the door, and two security guards entered to collect the man from the floor, careful to avoid the drool dripping from his parted lips.

"Before you start, may I show you something?" the boss asked Miranda.

"Sure."

"I still don't get it?" Midnite asked.

"Of course you don't, sweetie," Miranda replied with a sympathetic glint in her eyes.

"Why this charade today? Why have Trick here on the tour if that was all that you wanted?"

"Because I had to be sure that Trick was a good choice. I like breaking egotistical men, especially ones who think they're better than women. This was proof that Trick was exactly what I wanted in a specimen. Also, it was fun playing with my gift. Mental torture can be worse than physical torture. When Trick wakes up, he'll be asking himself the same questions, and not have any answers."

Midnite shrugged. "I guess. Okay. You still need me around, boss?"

He told her that the choice was hers, but Miranda asked her to tag along.

A SHORT
POINTLESS WALK

They made their way to a dark basement.

"This exhibit we'll only walk past because I'm unsure what to do with it yet," the boss explained. "It's all good fun, and I'm sure we'll come up with something, though. Our main destination is the room after this one. I can't wait for Miranda to see my surprise."

This time, they entered the room instead of watching through a window. A stench invaded their olfactory senses.

The walls were wide, the ceilings high.

Dozens of high-pitched voices yelled out. 'Help us!', 'please', and "let us go" were some of the words heard.

"I call this my garden of women," the boss hit a switch, and a bright light illuminated the room. "But, as you can see, well partially see, it's actually an inground pool."

Miranda and Midnite had to look down towards their feet to get the full picture, but there were heads on the floor, some sort of large pool cover with various holes cut through it and locked around their necks, hiding their bodies.

"As I was saying, it's an inground pool, their bodies are safely rotting beneath, standing in their own bodily fluids. That pool cover is especially designed to lock them in place. They can move their bodies beneath the unseen surface, but they're not close enough to touch each other, and there's nothing down there for them to touch. And they can basically do is stand, or if they get tired, they can rest their body weight on their necks and the solid pool cover, which can be painful to the cervical vertebrae."

"What?" Midnite asked. "Bodily fluids?"

"Yes. Feces. Urine. Menstrual blood. The pool ranges from five feet in depth to six feet, and they're placed accordingly for their height."

"This is like an evil genius thing to do," Miranda said, with amusement. "Why?"

The boss shrugged. "Why not? My own curiosity. Curious to see how long it will take for them to fill the pool. That's not a bad idea. I wonder how long until their own filth infects their bodies? Do you think that's deadly?"

Midnite pinched her nose. "I'm not sure if it's deadly, but it sure reeks."

"I'll think of something," the boss said, opening the door and ushering them out.

"Imagine doing something like that on reality television. Willing participants, though, and see who lasts the longest." Miranda's usually quiet and squeaky voice was now loud and motivated. "It'd be gross, and I'm sure viewers would love it. We could livestream it, on a legit portion of the internet though, just like that TV show that has people living in the same house. The one where they only air a few hours a week on television, but the internet shows their every movement and every word spoken every single day. Of course the CDC would be strict about medical care and food and whatnot, but if people willingly opt to use the restroom on themselves to win, say, cash or a car or something, then I bet we could work something out."

The boss gave her a wink. "You have your father's creative mind. I think we'll do some great business together. C'mon, I have something else to show you."

BLAKE THE
BROKEN MAN

"This next one is my personal pride and joy," the boss boasted. "Not much to look at. Won't contribute much to the zoo. He's more like my personal pet project."

Inside the window was a man.

Four metal shackles locked around each limb, heavy chains trailing from each wrist and ankle, making a pathway across the concrete floor, disappearing into holes on the lowest parts of the walls.

The man's face hadn't been torn apart and reapplied, but a thick, long beard covered him from cheek to chin. The hairs were dark with patches of gray, curled and matted.

Where his eyes used to be white were now red, giving him a devilish glow.

Wrinkles cascaded his forehead and eyes, an implication that the man was much older than the youthful tone of his body. Which was not muscular, but may have been at one point in his life, with loose folds of flesh hanging around his rib cages but somehow still tight in other places.

The man was seated, his back against a wall, his neck limp resting his head upon a shoulder. Legs spread, arms draped on both sides as if he was suffering from pure exhaustion.

Once he saw the trio of people staring into his empty room of a cage, the man's eyes looked from Midnite to Miranda to the boss.

He squinted, as if he didn't trust his own eyesight, but then a flash of recognition appeared as a scowl.

Immediately, with a sudden spark of energy, the man jumped from his seated position, both hands out in front of him as if reaching for the man on the other side of the window ready to strangle him through the glass.

The man's chains stretched as far as they could, and once they were overextended his body was snapped backward, haltering his motion.

The boss nodded towards a camera hidden beneath a black dome on the ceiling.

A large clinking noise escalated and the chains retracted towards their holes, further pulling the man. Each arm and leg in opposite directions, until the man's flesh and bone was taut, pulled firmly and suspended into the air.

Beneath his matted beard, the man opened his mouth, revealing neglected teeth, and he howled like an animal in pain.

Biceps and quadriceps bulged against the tension,

him trying to force his freedom from his metal bindings to reach the man he obviously hated.

"I'm calling this one Blake the Broken Man," the boss offered after the brief display of anguish.

"What does he do?" Midnite asked. "He's not even looking at me. Men always look at me."

"He hates me," the boss answered. "That's what he does. And for good reason. Through a domino ripple of cruelty, I ruined his life for no other reason than him being in the wrong place at the wrong time. Now this is just for my own amusement."

Chains clicked again, pulling Blake's arms behind him until both fists touched behind his back, pulling him downward. Both legs were shooting in opposite directions, spreading further apart towards the walls, making it impossible for him to stand.

The strobe lighting started, flashes between light and dark, offering only a momentary glimpse of the man's body being twisted and deformed.

The only thing that was still evident was the hatred in the man's eyes targeted towards the boss.

"He doesn't do much of anything, other than be tortured. I had high hopes for him, even offered him a job, but he refused. Now it's a game of how far I can destroy him and make him wish he never existed. I have a side similar to yours," the boss said with a slight nod towards Miranda. "I, too, like to play with people. I merely wanted to show you how similar we are, the same traits we possess where we must feel dominant."

The boss knew that Miranda understood what he

meant.

The lengths he went through to ensure he didn't judge her for tying men up for her own sexual and demented desires.

This made his offering of Trick to her feel even more special.

PART FOUR:
WHAT WE DO FOR
BUSINESS AND
ENTERTAINMENT

WHAT'S HAPPENIN'

The rope was a simple one, thick and rough.

The knots that circled his wrists were impossible, looping through itself several times.

The way his feet could barely touch the ground, forcing Trick to stand on the tips of his toes, or else the entirety of his body weight would apply more pressure to his wrists, which were now purple from being suspended so high above his head.

"Let me go! Do you know who I am?" Trick screamed into the darkness. "This has to be a mistake. I get it. This was fun and all, but please! It feels like my hands will fall off!"

His lungs inflated and deflated between words, the slight sway of movement enough to force him to straighten his posture and try to compensate and ease the dangling.

Behind him, he heard a noise, and Trick quickly turned around, the rope twisting with him and caused his foot to slip. His toes scrambled for traction and despite the fact the floor wasn't mobile, it felt like it was moving further away from him.

"Shhh."

The rope twisted again, facing him away from the sound of the feminine shush.

Like a mirage, the female approached him, standing before him, her hourglass shape barely a visible outline in the dark room. The only light was due to the door she left open behind them, only a slight bit of illumination.

"It's okay. Calm down," Midnite said, stepping closer towards him, her high heels clicking against the concrete floor. "You said you wanted me naked, right? Here I am."

Suddenly his mouth was dry and Trick found it hard to speak. "Ba–a-by," the word was longer than its two syllables. There was more he wanted to voice, but was too busy swallowing his pride due to his earlier begging and crying out for help.

"Do you like what you see?" she asked him, inches from his body, trailing her index finger down the buttons of his shirt.

Trick was glad it was dark so that she couldn't see the tears welled up in his eyes, but also wished for more light so that he could see her nude form. "Sure, let me down. I'll show you how much I like what I see."

"You aren't mad at me?" she asked, coyly, sucking on the finger that had just been on his chest. Reaching down, she grabbed his crotch area. "I guess you're not too mad."

Confused was an understatement. "You didn't have to tie me up. We could have done this anytime. Just untie me. I'll give you what you want. I can't feel my hands anymore."

Midnite dropped to her knees, not surprised that being strung up by his hands didn't prevent him from forming an erection. "Is this what you want?" she asked, slowly unzipping his black jeans. "My mouth on your hard cock?"

"Cut me down," Trick mumbled before finding strength in his voice. "Let me free, and I'll give you what you want. What is this? Some game? A joke? Okay. Let's do this."

"No underpants!" Midnite exclaimed loudly. "It bounced right out at me! Come in here! Look at this!"

"Who are you talking to?" Trick asked. "Who?"

Nobody came. Nobody responded.

"I guess nobody," Midnite said with a shrug.

The room did light up, giving Trick a better view of the sexy vixen, her breasts so close to his boner that he could imagine how great it would feel rubbing his dick between the two silicone (assumed) implants. "Wow! This sure is a great joke! Okay. I'm a good sport. Can we just do this?"

Midnite made a presentation of leaning forward to kiss the head of his shaft, but stopped just shy of her lips touching his flesh.

She wrapped her dainty fingers around his dick and allowed her long fingernails to graze his tender skin, and squeezed. "Do you like it rough?"

"Get me down, and I'll like it anyway you want to

give it to me."

"I told you this was pointless!" Midnite said too loud. "I'm done!"

In her haste to back away from the firm appendage dangling in front of her face, Midnite shoved his firm member against his hairless pubic area and started zipping his pants back up, not bothered that the sensitive skin of his penis was caught between the zipper teeth.

Quickly, she pulled the latch upwards and watched flesh bubble up between the metal in red, angry mounds. Tads of skin were ripped into wounds, specks of blood restrained by the pressure of the zippered constraints.

The meat sticking out from the zipper looked like bleeding blisters ready to pop at any moment.

"You're a jerk! You know that!" Midnite screamed, making sure his pants were zipped all the way up.

Miranda burst into the room. "You weren't supposed to hurt him! I just wanted you to see if he liked rough sex! Because if he did, I wouldn't torture him sexually!"

"Well, look at him," was Midnite's reply. "He doesn't enjoy it!"

Trick was dangling from the ropes, tears dripping down his cheeks, his legs quivering beneath him, swinging around trying to kick at the two women in the room. "Please! Make it stop!"

"I need his dick intact!" Miranda yelled. Not knowing what else to do, she unzipped the zipper, which in turn fully separated those patches of flesh from his body. "Actually, I think I can work with this!"

With a glint in her eye, Miranda pointed and laughed at the bits and portions of dick skin that were stuck in his lowered pants. "It looks like an overcooked hot dog! Split on one side, swollen on the others! I can have fun with this!"

For fun, she finagled her around his dangling body and then re-zipped up his pants, creating new tears and rips in his dick meat.

BEHIND CLOSED OFFICE DOORS

"I warned you about sending Midnite in there," the boss said. "Her heart is in the right place, but she's not the smartest. I hope you don't think her performance reflects how I conduct business."

"It was a long shot sending her in there. I have huge plans for Trick. What Dom doesn't want a womanizing douche bag like him as her Sub? It's truly a dream come true. It's a personal test of mine to see if I can break him. Tear him away from reality so that he loses himself in the process and forgets who he was before I took him."

The boss hated it that Miranda ignored his statement. "I made good on my end. Had Trick believing he'd be the host of our TV show. Lured him here. Now he's in there swinging like a busted cryin' piñata. Here's my question for you. You're a Dahmer. Your father was a legend. Why me to help you with your television venture?"

"That's easy. I'm an admirer of your work, and

needed someone I can trust with my deviant side. Of course, I'll be strictly professional when creating the shows, because television is not the dark web. So many rules and regulations. I guess my question is why do you want to be involved with my show?"

"Fame. I love what I do here, but I do it without recognition. Which is better than going to prison. I want more. Something else. Not sure if this will scratch that itch, but I think it'll be fun finding out."

"Anything else before I leave?"

"No. I'll be in touch. I'll have a couple of my security guys help you get him back to your house. Unless your plans are to keep him here? I wouldn't mind that one bit. I wouldn't interfere with what you do to him. I might look in from time-to-time. Same as I do with Blake the Broken Man. Mementos I enjoy most."

PART FIVE: GRATUITOUS

NEW FRIENDS

Midnite was shocked to get a knock on her dressing room door. "You're still here?"

Seeing Miranda was a pleasant surprise.

"I might stick around for a day or two. I'm sorry how Trick treated you today."

"I think I got even by zipping his willy into tatters. It's nothing I can't handle. I think seeing you in that room with him changed my thoughts about you."

Miranda bit her bottom lip and neared the few feet gap between her and her internet idol. "What did you think of me?"

"I thought you were too quiet. Shy, I guess. At first, I thought maybe you were spoiled because of who your dad is. But now I see that I was wrong. You're stronger than I expected. You were thrilled watching that prick suffer."

"You're not as dumb as some people think."

"Who thinks I'm dumb?"

"Trick, for one person, I guess."

"Do you think I'm stupid?"

Miranda focused on Midnite's mouth and not her words. "No, I don't. And you're beautiful. You did me a favor with Trick all day, and I'm indebted to you."

"All day? Oh. I wasn't sure what was happening other than the tour."

"Did hurting him turn you on like it did me?"

"Huh? Maybe."

The silence was inviting. Comfortable. A short-lived moment that bonded two lonely people, both confined by their lifestyles and occupations that left the both of them feeling like outsiders to society.

Miranda was the first to speak. "You understand?"

"I think so."

Without warning, Miranda leaned forward and planted her mouth on Midnite's soft, plump lips.

Miranda pulled away. "Is that okay?"

Midnite softly stroked Miranda's cheek, which was the complete opposite of what they both usually experienced. The touch was sensual, not tortuous. Meaningful. Intimate, even if it wasn't sexual.

"How do you feel, after seeing the zoo today?" Midnite asked.

"Alive. Exhilarated. Yearning." Miranda was accustomed to hurting her subjects, whether they were willing or not. She had her own gimps over time, and now Trick would become one that she owned. Still, she wanted something more.

"I'm wet," Midnite whispered.

Miranda wasted no time pressing her body against the other woman, their breasts on level, nipple to nipple. Midnite's boobs rose above the cut of her bustier.

Within moments, they both scrambled, each

undressing themselves in a rush to feel the warmth of another's body that understood how they felt.

They found their way to Midnite's bed, lying side by side, mouth-to-mouth. Tit to tit. Their legs intertwined like a twisted pretzel, dough forming to each other's shape.

Miranda touched the moist spot between Midnite's legs, gently, and then brought her finger to her mouth to taste the delicate juice.

A thunderous, abrupt knock on Midnite's dressing room door killed the moment and pulled them from their lustful trance.

"Yes!" Midnite hollered. "Who is it?"

"It's me. Are you busy?"

ALWAYS ON
THE JOB

Miranda, feeling equal to her business partner and new lover, didn't feel the need to cover up as Midnite answered the door.

The boss didn't enter the room, but his voice was loud enough to feel like he was in the same space. "You ready for some voiceovers? Maybe some edits? Some posing in front of a few of the zoo exhibits so we can put this commercial together? I'd really like to get this promo started."

Midnite's nudity was nothing new for her employer to see, and she also felt no shame in not being covered. "Sure."

"Can I come?"

"Who's that in there?" the boss snaked his neck around so that he could see past Midnite. "Oh. Hey. I never thought when I assigned you a room next door to the Madam's that you'd end up in here. Forget about the promo tonight."

"Actually, I'd like to get your okay, that is if Midnite

wants to, that me and her could go spend some time with Trick?"

The boss was shocked at Miranda's question. "You're not a slave here. You have freedom to roam, and so does Madam Midnite. Do as you wish. Allowing you rooms when you stay here is just for convenience, and not for my own authority over you."

Both women were excited about another visit to the sexist comedian.

SEXY TIME

Trick was still dangling from the ropes, both hands above his head.

His pants, the groin area still zipped up with bulging dick meat sticking out through the metal zipper teeth. Blood had saturated the material, painting the front of his pants a dark red color.

The moment they entered and turned on the light, Trick's voice echoed around the room. A plea for help and to be cut down. "Please help me."

Since they entered behind him, he couldn't see who they were.

Once they came into his view, Trick's eyes darted open. From where he had been crying, crust had developed between his upper and lower eyelid corners. His cheeks were flushed red. Hands were now a deeper purple from lack of blood flow.

Miranda stood back and stared, a tingle growing between her legs. "I think I'll have lots of fun with this one. What do you think?"

"I know I can have fun with him," Midnite said, disrobing, showing her glorious female form. "Do you think he can get hard like that?"

Miranda shrugged. "Doubt it. Ask him. His dick looks broken to me, at least what I can see of it. How about this? If you get hard, I'll cut you down."

"This is insane!" Trick cried. "I'm sorry! I'm so sorry!"

"Yes, you are," Miranda replied, "but not as sorry as you're going to be."

"Did you mention something earlier about me sucking your dick?" Midnite asked. "How about I make that fantasy come true?"

Madam Midnite dropped to her knees, and Trick's body tensed up in remembrance of the pain she gifted him earlier when she had been in that exact same pose. His legs were so atrophied from standing on the tips of his toes that even trying to kick was nearly impossible.

Midnite kept her eyes on Miranda, but brought her lush lips closer to the bits of ruined cock skin swelling through the zipper.

"That's so hot," Miranda said, sucking on her finger.

Lips spread wide, head turned sideways, Midnite used her teeth and tongue to tease what small portion of his dick was visible.

"Stop! Stop! No!"

The moment built, tensions growing larger by the second.

Midnite's teeth widened, welcoming the bloodied, ruined man meat into her mouth. Her teeth clamped down in a fury and scraped off a thin scab that had started to form.

"No! NO! NO!"

"Yes, yes, yes," Miranda moaned.

Fresh blood on her lips like wild lipstick, Midnite teased her lover from a distance and sensually licked at the sticky fluid, making a show of how skilled she was at using her mouth.

Miranda's hand reached out for her new lover, grabbing her by the hair and pulling her lips close to her own crotch.

Through the thin fabric of Miranda's panties, Midnite could smell the earthy scent of a woman in heat. A woman needing to be touched.

The silk felt good against her tongue, Trick's blood meshing with the soft cloth, creating a coppery taste of lust.

Trick's body flailed, his legs pushing the two women away from him, but they were so caught up in the moment that they barely noticed.

"Let's see if he can get hard," Miranda teased, bent over, her hand on the zipper.

In a flash, she pulled downward like ripping off a band-aid, but instead it was metal teeth breaking tender flesh away from a man's sex shaft.

His dick was now freed from captivity, no jeans holding it against his body.

The loose appendage dangled between his legs in a limp gesture of frailty.

In any other circumstance, watching a woman inhale another's vagina scent through her mouth would have excited him, but blood trickling from his fresh wounds proved that he wasn't up to the task of being aroused.

Lost in their own world of pleasure, the women got wetter the louder his screams became.

Midnite took a second to glance at the final product of their torture.

The sight of the ruined sex organ only got her hotter. One side of the glans was nothing but ribbons of thin skin. The majority of the penis was turning purple and swollen with pain.

Miranda gave her new gimp a reminder. "If you get hard, I'll cut you down."

Trick knew that it was an impossible task.

What used to be the favorite part of his body was now destroyed beyond recognition, with no function.

SMALL SLICE OF PROMOTIONAL COMMERCIAL

Mouth still painted red with Trick's dick blood, the boss had a cameraman filming the sexy vixen in front of a zoo exhibit that Miranda hadn't seen yet.

"I do like watching her work," Miranda confessed.

"Yes," the boss agreed. "She's something else. A perfect form and a pliable brain, easy to influence. If you enjoy this, I'll have a treat after we wrap up this scene."

Miranda was now wearing a silk robe that covered her from neck to knee, and her hard nipples were evident through the thin fabric. Aware of herself, and in comparison to her business partner still wearing a suit, she wrapped her arms around her body. "Is this too informal?"

The boss nodded towards the other woman. "She's in there, completely nude with the exception of some spiked heels. We're really casual around here."

"In the TV business, it will be completely different. Professional clothing only."

"I'm very aware."

In front of them, Midnite was posing for the camera.

With the cameraman's direction, she did as she was told.

'Squeeze your breasts'

'Pinch your nipples'

'Lie down on your back and spread your legs'

"On your knees, finger between your lips'

"On your knees, rump up, facing me'

In each shot, behind her was the main focus of the camera lens, which was the zoo exhibit.

"You know how cameras work? Right? We'll edit this up, chop it up like short subliminal messages. The zoo is still a work in progress, but this will motivate the viewers to watch a stream or two-"

The boss' words were cut off by Jack violently slamming his nude body into the bulletproof glass separating him from Midnite who was teasing him with her nude curves.

Jack, proving himself to be a true animal, was slobbering from his mouth, as he dry humped the glass to try in hopes of providing relief to his medicinal-enhanced erection.

His cock was squished between the lowest part of his abdomen and the clear barrier, to the point that his sex organ was turning purple. Like an animal in heat, he writhed against the glass, his hands continuously trying to reach out for Midnite. His cock pulsed and throbbed visibly until he climaxed, spewing his sticky sex juice on the glass.

"Get a great shot of that," the boss directed the cameraman. "The more barbaric, the better. Show the viewers how our animals act. How much entertainment they might provide."

"His face...". Midnite stopped herself from speaking, afraid she wouldn't properly verbalize her thoughts.

"Oh yeah, just skin cut away, reattached, like a jigsaw puzzle. Very sterile with thorough medical supervision, I assure you."

"Oh, I don't doubt that."

"Now, after this, maybe we can brainstorm new ideas. For this. For other projects. For the reality television show. After I show you something very special to me."

WATCHING A WOMAN WORK

Midnite was no stranger to allowing herself to be subjected to a man's libido.

Teasing Jack was one thing.

Blake the Broken Man was something else altogether.

In a creepier way.

This man wasn't barbaric or animalistic.

With cold, black eyes, Blake watched Midnite finger herself, but neither his dick nor his face responded with any change.

"See how blank he is?" The boss asked. "That's my pride and joy. I took a perfectly healthy man, and turned him into nothing. Less than nothing. A shell of an existence."

"How?" Miranda asked, her more interested in watching Blake's blank stare instead of Midnite's sexy body. "What'd you do to him?"

"The how isn't what's important. It's the why. I like to think of him as myself in reverse. The weaker he gets, the stronger I get."

Miranda nodded in agreement. "I do understand. How I feel when I torture one of my sex slaves, or drain their blood to paint upon a pure white canvass. There's something therapeutic about that. Strength. Power."

"This is why I think we'll make a great business team. Okay, Madam, you can stop now. You've made my point."

Midnite pulled her voluptuous breast away from the glass window. "Okay."

"Do you by chance track your cycles?" Miranda asked her.

"My cycle?" Midnite didn't know what she was asking about.

"Your monthly? Your woman time."

"Oh yeah. Why?"

"I have a feeling your menstrual blood could make some great art."

The boss smiled, proud of his new business partner, knowing that his future was about to get very interesting.

A NOTE FROM
MY DARK MIND

People are animals in a sense. In the way that we're mammals according to the animal kingdom. We share DNA with primates... blah, blah, blah... I'm sure we were all aware of those facts. I'm not here to teach a science lesson.

So is it a stretch to have a human zoo?

Historically, there were zoos of people (described as public displays of people in a so-called natural (primate) state). Those were bad... Not nice... Once again, I'm not here to teach a history lesson...

My version of a people zoo is horrible. If it were a real life thing, I'd be against it.

With it being a fictional thing, that's a totally different story.

Fiction is an escape from reality. I like to keep the majority of my stories so that they could happen in real life. Could this happen? Sure.

But it's inhumane. Cruel. Wrong.

I feel the need to literally write those words because apparently some people judge fictional writers by the context that we write... We are not what we write.

In a perfect world, I wouldn't have to clarify how wrong it would be to hold humans captive and force them into zoos. I would like to think it would go without saying.

+++

On another note, have you ever watched a video of a facelift? The way the surgeon makes incisions around the face, and then tucks and sucks away fat cells and loose skin and all that other medical jargon? It's gross.

Inside, we're all made of the same stuff. And I believe our outsides are much prettier than what we're comprised of inside. Or is it the other way around? Is there some sort of beauty to what lies beneath our flesh?

Watching a facelift video was how I got the idea to hide the 'animals' faces by cutting away their flesh, only to reattach it randomly in patches. If you can visually picture it in your brain (the same way I did), it's not a pretty sight. Possibly some might say it's a disturbing image. Possibly other people wouldn't.

So many things are a matter of opinion.

Who noticed that I brought in not 1, not 2, not 3, not 4, but 5 characters from other books? Some of my stories are evolving within the same fictional universe. I've tried to write each story so that you don't have to read the other stories for everything to make sense, and also to not give away spoilers.

Here's the list of characters...

1 the boss (obviously because it's his world, I merely write it)(from Found Bag of doom, Circus For the Rich, and My Vagina Smells Like Sulfur)

2 Madam Midnite (from My Vagina Smells like Sulfur)

3 Miranda (from Deadly Reality TV and she also made a small appearance in Raised by a Killer)

4 Trick (from Punched Line)

5 and Blake (from Found Bag of Doom)

Trick is my least favorite character to write. Sexist jokes are not my style. However, it made him the character that he is. Is it strange that I don't mind writing violence but anything misogynist makes me cringe? Does that make me a complex and complicated person?

On the flip side, Miranda wanted the ultimate alpha male that she can break down slowly but surely. There might be more of that to come in other stories....

Do we have any thoughts on the human zoo?

This is just a story. Fictional. For entertainment purposes.

Good thing it's fiction..... Nothing here to psychoanalyze. My only hope is that it entertained you. If so, I consider my job done. If I didn't entertain you, so very sorry.

If you liked this story, I have plenty of other titles available to read...

Stay dark my friends.
Until next time.

If you're like me and don't spend much time on social media, here's a good old fashioned email. sharoncheatham81@gmail.com. Do you have any questions, comments, complaints, or compliments? I'd love to hear from you.

I read often and love Goodreads, too. If you want to keep up with what I'm reading, I'm Sea Caummisar on Goodreads.

Until then, Stay Dark My Friends,
See ya next read,
Your Friend,
Sea Caummisar
Contact Info for Sea Caummisar
Facebook (Sea Caummisar)
Twitter (@seacaummisar)
Goodreads (Sea Caummisar)

See ya next read

Printed in Great Britain
by Amazon

47701295R00067